Seasons

Autumn

Siân Smith

www.raintreepublishers.co.uk
Visit our website to find out more information about Raintree books.

To order:

☎ Phone 0845 6044371

🗎 Fax +44 (0) 1865 312263

✉ Email myorders@capstonepub.co.uk

Customers from outside the UK please telephone +44 1865 312262

Raintree is an imprint of Capstone Global Library Limited, a company incorporated in England and Wales having its registered office at 7 Pilgrim Street, London, EC4V 6LB – Registered company number: 6695582

Raintree is a registered trademark of Pearson Education Limited, under licence to Capstone Global Library Limited

Edited by Rebecca Rissman, Charlotte Guillain, and Siân Smith
Designed by Joanna Hinton-Malivoire
Picture research by Elizabeth Alexander and Sally Claxton
Production by Duncan Gilbert
Originated by Heinemann Library
Printed and bound in China by South China Printing Company Ltd

ISBN 978 0 431 19280 2 (hardback)
13 12 11 10 09
10 9 8 7 6 5 4 3 2 1

ISBN 978 0 431 19285 7 (paperback)
14 13 12 11 10
10 9 8 7 6 5 4 3 2 1

British Library Cataloguing in Publication Data
Smith, Siân
Autumn. - (Seasons)
1. Autumn - Juvenile literature
I. Title
508.2

Acknowledgements
The author and publisher are grateful to the following for permission to reproduce copyright material: ©Alamy pp.**10, 11** (Blend Images), **20** (David Norton), **9** (Judy Freilicher), **14, 23 bottom** (Neil Dangerfield), **8** (Phill Lister), **16** (Renee Morris), **21** (Silksatsunrise Photography); ©Corbis pp.**22** (Craig Tuttle), **04 br** (Image100), **17** (Tetra Images), **04 tl** (Zefa/Roman Flury); ©GAP Photos pp.**18, 23 top** (Fiona Lea); ©Getty Images pp.**04 tr** (Floria Werner), **5** (Philippe Renault); ©iStockphoto.com pp.**6, 23 middle** (Bojan Tezak), **04 bl** (Inga Ivanova); ©Photodisc p.**12** (Photolink); ©Photolibrary p.**13** (Chad Ehlers), **15** (J-Charles Gerard/Photononstop); ©Punchstock p.**7** (Brand X Pictures/Morey Milbradt); ©Shutterstock p.**19** (Vakhrushev Pavel).

Cover photograph of maple tree reproduced with permission of ©Shutterstock (Tatiana Grozetskaya). Back cover photograph reproduced with permission of ©Photodisc (Photolink).

Contents

What is autumn?

spring

summer

autumn

winter

There are four seasons every year.

Autumn is one of the four seasons.

When is autumn?

spring

summer

winter

autumn

The four seasons follow a pattern.

Autumn comes after summer.

The weather in autumn

It can be chilly in autumn.

It can be foggy in autumn.

What can we see in autumn?

In autumn we can see people
in jumpers.

In autumn we can see people
in coats.

In autumn we can see coloured
leaves on trees.

In autumn we can see coloured
leaves on the ground.

In autumn we can see seeds.

In autumn we can see fruits
and vegetables.

In autumn we can see berries.

In autumn we can see pumpkins.

In autumn we can see bonfires.

In autumn we can see fireworks.

In autumn we can see animals carrying food.

In autumn we can see birds
flying away.

Which season comes next?

Which season comes after autumn?

Picture glossary

bonfire outdoor fire

pattern happening in the same order

seed plants make seeds. Seeds grow into new plants.

Index

Notes for parents and teachers
Before reading
Listen to a few minutes of *Autumn* from Vivaldi's *Four Seasons*. Tell the children to close their eyes and think about the following images of autumn: leaves changing colour, leaves falling from the trees, the lights coming on in the evenings, the different clothes they put on to keep warm, squirrels collecting nuts. Ask them what they like best about the autumn.

After reading
- Make a garland of leaves. You will need: enough leaves from different trees for each child to have one leaf; paper, pencils, crayons, scissors, long piece of string. Make a collection of different shapes of leaves and show the children. Tell them to select a leaf and to draw it on a piece of paper with a thick stem. They should then mark the veins and cut out their leaf. Fold the stem in half and attach it to the string. Suspend the string of leaves across the classroom.
- Make a zig-zag book. You will need: A4 paper folded lengthways and then cut in half (making two long rectangles). Fold the length in half and then half again. Unfold the strip and bend the creases to make the book zig-zag. Give each child a zig-zag book and tell them to draw a different thing on each page that reminds them of autumn. Display the books in the classroom.